Baptista Mantuanus, Sebastian Evans

John Baptist Spagnolo of Mantua Carmelite

to John Crestoni of Piacenza Carmelite then going away for a time to Monte

Calestano

Baptista Mantuanus, Sebastian Evans

John Baptist Spagnolo of Mantua Carmelite
to John Crestoni of Piacenza Carmelite then going away for a time to Monte Calestano

ISBN/EAN: 9783741115059

Manufactured in Europe, USA, Canada, Australia, Japa

Cover: Foto ©Andreas Hilbeck / pixelio.de

Manufactured and distributed by brebook publishing software
(www.brebook.com)

Baptista Mantuanus, Sebastian Evans

John Baptist Spagnolo of Mantua Carmelite

JOHN BAPTIST SPAGNOLO OF MANTUA CARMELITE
TO JOHN CRESTONI OF PIACENZA CARMELITE
THEN GOING AWAY FOR A TIME
TO MONTE CALESTANO

ENGLISHED WITH AN INTRODUCTION BY
SEBASTIAN EVANS

TWENTY-FIVE COPIES PRIVATELY PRINTED AS
NEW-YEAR GIFTS MDCCCLXXXIV.

L'Envoy.

Enter! The cell is bare and spare,
   Yet in this narrow domicil
   An Anchoret of Carmel Hill
Found room of old for more than prayer.
See, here beside his scapulaire
   Is left upon the casement-sill,
   (Downy with dust, yet fragrant still.
A perfume-jar of Mantuan ware.

A few crisp immortelles at top
   Are clustered less for smell than show,
   But warm and rich the scents below —
Rare petals of clove-gilliver,
   Dried roses, spikes of lavender,
Bud heads, still sweet, of heliotrope.

                S.E.

INTRODUCTION.

OUR Natural Philosophers do hold that the famous fair white marble of Carrara, and for aught I know that of Paros and Pentelicus to boot, was in the original thereof nought but a common limestone, sublimed by the heat of huge masses of molten granite thrust upward in some fiery throe within the womb of Mother Earth. This heat, say they, did not only bake, as it were, and in part calcine the neighbouring rock, but did also permeate, purify, and impregnate the substance thereof with certain fumes and fluxes and solvents and concretives, which, by the help of I know not what co-operant magnetick and electrick energies, wrought in the lapse of ages a perfect transmutation and metamorphosis; whereby it came to pass that a coarse rock—otherwise unfit for any but a stone-fence mason, and worthy at best to burn for mortar—hath by Plutonick alchemy become the pure white crystalline matrix, according to that old Platonick conceit, wherein the carver of statues—Mr. Hamo Thorney-croft, let me say, for instance—may find the fairest and most divine of those presences his genius can in idea conceive. A like change, methinks, was wrought in the world, not of matter, but of mind, by the New Birth of Art and Letters in the fifteenth and sixteenth centuries. Indeed, as Mr. Victor Hugo intimateth in his fantastical poem of The Satyr, the intellectual history of the Modern World is but little more than the record of the transformations wrought by the subtile and far-reaching effluences and influences of that New Birth. But, leaving Generals to others—for, indeed, the story of what the French, and we after the French, call the Renaissance, were a burden as far beyond my power as my intent—I know not whether the Poem here Englished be not as good an example as may be found of the theologick speculation of the Middle Ages, sublimated into a material

In the Legend of the Centuries.

far more precious through having lain very nigh to those hypogæan masses of humanist granite, fluid with the heat of the very core of our globe, which seethed and heaved under Italy four hundred years ago. The original Latin elegiacks are, if I mistake not, true metamorphick marble—if not of Carrara, yet of Mantua; and the workman who fashioned them, if not a John of Bologna or a Pisan John or Nicholas, hath yet the hand of no common master.

For, indeed, though he hath been held but of little account this long time past, the inditer of the verses, John Baptist Spagnolo, the Mantuan, was deservedly of no small note in his day, and for no small space thereafter. As his name, Spagnolo, betokeneth, he came of Spanish stock, his grandfather, one Antony of Cordova, being to all appearance the first of the family to settle in Italy. Be this as it may, Peter Spagnolo, son of Antony, was a gentleman of some consideration (like enough a merchant who had made money) living in Mantua in 1448, the year our Baptist was born to him, though 'tis question whether by his wife, Constance de' Maggi, of Brescia. Paul Jovius, ever of a curst and biting humour, save where he was minded for vanity or lucre to flatter, saith that Baptist was born *ex damnato coitu*. On the other hand, Father Lawrence Cupaer, who edited his works, in his introductory epistle denounceth Jovius for a slanderer. The controversy may be seen in the Menagiana, where Mr. Ménage taketh the part of Jovius, partly on the ground that Jovius, born not far from Mantua, and thirty-three years old when Baptist died, might well have known the truth. But, seeing that the same Jovius saith that Baptist was over eighty when he died, whereas in truth he was not yet seventy, 'tis clear that the splenetick bishop, however excellent his opportunities, took no great pains to discover the truth. Nevertheless, Mr. Ménage's other arguments are more valid, and he leaveth it more likely that Baptist, among many other great men, was a bastard. But be this so or not, 'tis certain that he was recognized by his father as his son, and that his brothers—whose legitimacy hath never been called in question—Ptolemy, Giles, Frederick, and Alexander, were proud to claim their kindred with him. If, as seemeth beyond question, the Pollux of his 7th Eclogue be but another name for Baptist himself, his father would seem to have dealt somewhat hardly with him in his boyhood—*immitis*

In Italian—Giovan Battista, or Giambattista, or Battista Spagnolo, or Spagnuolo, Mantovano. In Latin—Joannes Baptista Hispaniolus, Mantuanus, or briefly Baptista Mantuanus. In French—Commonly Battiste de Mantoue. In English—Commonly plain Mantuan.

Elog. Doct. Vir. lxi.

J. B. Mantuani Opera. Antwerp, 1576; 4 vols., 8vo.

Vol. I., p. 275, ed. Paris, 1729.

pater—yet 'tis to his father he dedicates his tractate, *de Vitâ Beatâ*, and when he cometh to mention him in poems writ after he came to manhood, 'tis with something more than respect, if somewhat short of enthusiastic affection. For his brother Ptolemy—who, becoming of the household of Francis of Gonzaga, took the family name of Gonzaga, and who married Dorothy de' Valenti—he wrote an epithalamium, and also dedicated to him his dialogue, *Contra Detractores*, in which his brother Alexander appeareth as one of the interlocutors. This Ptolemy Gonzaga, also, took up the cudgels on behalf of his brother against the criticks, whom he belaboureth—in Latine as questionable as Mantuan's own—with much vigour to little result.

As soon as he was of a fit age, Baptist took the cowl among the Carmelite Religious of the Congregation of Mantua, and from this time forth the history of his life is little more than a catalogue of his works and a register of the offices he held in his Order. Six different times, 'tis said, he was appointed Vicar-General, and in 1513 was—somewhat against his will, it would seem—made General of the Carmelites, in which office he died on March 20, 1516, when the great Saint who was to restore the Order to more than its elder fame—Theresa—was not yet quite a year old. In many of the titles of his works he is styled *Theologus*, but I know not precisely the significance of the word as thus applied. By an ordinance of the Council of Basle, in 1431, it had been decided that Cathedral Churches should have a *Theologus* to teach the priests and others in sacred letters and things pertaining to the cure of souls, as had been aforetime provided for in Metropolitan Churches by a statute of the General Lateran Council ; and I think it not unlikely that this office—in connection, maybe, with the Cathedral of Mantua or Bologna, or, it may well be, in connection with his own Congregation of White Friars—is thus denoted.

The dyspeptick and dyslogistick Jovius throughout his elogy hath not a word of eulogy for our Baptist. "He fell," saith he "on days in which there was no room for middling poets, yet he nevertheless found a rival in Cantalicius ;" as if he should say, "This man was a very Bavius, and like Bavius, had his Mævius." 'Tis enough praise, he proceedeth, for this Carmelite that he drank wholesomely of the fountains of Andes, neglected by his fellow-citizens of fifteen centuries ; though, he addeth—

referring, belike, to a shameful çento made from Virgil's verses by certain other Mantuans—'twas a fatal hint which revealed the sources of that more limpid Virgilian water of Andes to the brothers Lælius and Hippolytus Capilupi. He then of his charity writeth: " He died, over eighty, at Mantua, not altogether happy, inasmuch as in the last act of his life he was obliged to write a defence against his criticks, who had not indeed thumbed his poems, but had lamentably scored them with damnatory marks."

An error already noted.

Obeliscis non manibus miseré confodissent.

" On the death of the holy man and poet "—'tis still the Bishop who speaks—" the hooded priests of that Order paid long-winded tribute to his memory, but Prince Frederick "—for Jovius is too nice a Latinist to call Frederick Gonzaga, the second of that name, Marquis of Mantua, by so barbarous a title as *Marchio*—" erected a marble effigy of him, with a laurel crown, which is to be seen in a stone arch near the bust of Virgil—a pious juxtaposition verily, were it less ridiculous." Thus far this ecclesiastick slanderer, who methinks held it a note of the higher culture to scoff at those pioneers of letters whose sweat and blood had been spent like water to make the higher culture possible to them that came after. But he doth not allow even himself the last word, for he quoteth two disparaging epigrams on this odious comparison by Myrteus and Latomus, for dyslogy in such a case was indeed as easy as 'twas inevitable. In the latter of these Latomus writeth:

Alter Maro, alter Mantuanus est,

whereby I am reminded that our own honoured and to be honoured Laureate, in his late elogy of the divine Maro, dubbeth him by the style and title of *Mantovano*, which, sure, is strange, for though he were in very truth *Mantuanus*, yet was he never for no Latine nor English tongues nor ears *Mantovano*, as was our Baptist. Nor was even he the only poetick *Battista Mantovano*, for I have seen in the Bodleian a poem, intituled *Cæna saluberrima*, printed by Joce Badius in 1508, writ by one Baptista Fiæra Mantuanus, *medicus*, saith the title-page, *peritissimus et litteratissimus*.

Mantua me genuit, &c.

Dict. Historique, s. v. Batiste Spagnoli.

But to go back to our own Mantuan. Mr. Moreri reporteth, and I dare say not incorrectly, that Baptist was the author of 55,000 verses, all

of them, I take it, in Latine. Lilio Giraldi, moreover, doth justly pro- Dial. de Poet., quoted by Father Cupaer and others.
nounce him rather an *improvvisatore* than a ripe poet; indeed, his *Gradus*
ad Parnassum epithetes, synonymes, and periphrases, and his *Polyanthea* Extemporaneus magis quam maturus poeta.
thoughts and imagery, do show but too clearly that verse-making had
early become with him a mechanick exercise, for which he possessed an
apparatus that did grind out Latine metre with most infelicitous rapidity
and ease.

That this disastrous facility should make much that he writ worth-
less was inevitable; and his interminable Lives of the Saints, masculine
and feminine, and suchlike pious superfluities, since life itself is short,
can never, sure, have been worth reading to any mortal who knew what
life is worth. But that which hath been of most prejudice to his good
esteem among men of learning and spirit is the marvellous esteem in
which his juvenile Eclogues were held for so many years among pedants
and pedagogues and pretenders to learning. These Eclogues—of which
he himself was half ashamed, and to which, when he republished them
with revisions, after he had taken the cowl, he gave the title *Adolescentia*,
as if he would so acknowledge their imperfections, yet therewithal
extenuate them on the plea of youth— did for some reason, hard in these
latter days to conceive, so tickle the taste of scholasticks as to become,
and remain for some six or seven generations at least, one of the com-
monest text-books for tiros in Latine to thumb in well-nigh all the
grammar schools of Europe.

Master Alexander Barclay, while still monk of Ely, Englished
certain of Baptist's Lives of the Saints, and thus speaketh of him in the
Prologe to his Egloges, which, according to Mr. Warton, were writ History of English Poetry, Ed. London, 1824, IV., 247, where see more, though incorrect.
about 1514. After naming the "famous Theocrite" and the "moste
noble Virgill," Barclay writeth:

> And in like maner nowe lately in our dayes Ed. 1570, printed at the end of the Ship of Fooles.
> Hath other Poetes attempted the same wayes:
> As the most famous Baptist Mantuan
> The best of that sort since Poetes first began,
> And Frauncis Petrarke also in Italy
> In like maner stile wrote playne and meryly.

But if one would know exactly the esteem in which our Author was
held at the time Master Shakspere writ his *Love's Labour's Lost*, 'tis

easy to gather from the speech he putteth into the mouth of Holofernes, in which that sententious pedagogue quoteth the first line of Baptist's Eclogues :

Act IV., Sc. 2.

Fauste, precor gelidâ quando pecus omne sub umbrâ
Ruminat—and so forth.   Ah, good old Mantuan I I may speak of thee as the
    traveller doth of Venice :—

Vinegia, Vinegia,
Chi non te vede, non te pregia.

Old Mantuan, old Mantuan ! Who understandeth thee not, loves thee not.

On which passage Mr. Malone noteth that a translation of Mantuanus, by George Turberville, was printed in 8vo in 1563, and quoteth from Nashe's Apologie of Pierce Pennilesse, 1593 :

With the first and seconde leafe he plaies very prettilie, and in ordinarie terms of extenuating, verdits Pierce Pennilesse for a grammar-school wit ; saies his margine is as deeply learned as *Fauste, precor gelidâ.*

London, 1615.

Master Farnaby, moreover, in the preface to his edition of Martial's epigrams, complaineth that *ipsis pædagogulis Fauste, precor gelidâ sonet altius quam Arma virumque cano.*   And that these Eclogues continued to be taught in certain schools to a yet much later date is sufficiently instanced by the publication of a school edition of them at Cologne in

Ex officinâ Meyeri-ana, 8vo, with a por-trait of the author, ill-cut on copper, seemingly from a poor copy of a fine original.

1688, a copy whereof I have of the gift of my excellent good friend, Mr. Joseph Knight.   There is also, as I learnt by some lost or mislaid Bookseller's Catalogue, a translation into English verse of these Eclogues some time, I think, in the first half of the eighteenth century.

Now that one opening peradventure these Juvenilia should incontinent conclude that they held no matter to detain a latter-day reader, and that their author could show scant cause why posterity should stay execution of oblivion as to any other of his works, is exceeding likely, and it may well be doubted whether Master Shakspere or Schoolmaster Farnaby· knew much more about our Mantuan than the one poor line they quote, which, I take it, was even more lamentably hackneyed than

Theodule.

the *Æthiopum terras* of an earlier author.   Yet so to conclude would be less correct than logical, for, as I hope some day to show, there are sundry other poems of Mantuan's beside the one here presented which are far from wanting in modern interest, and notably the one intituled

1. Sixtus IV.

Alphonsus, of which Mr. Bayle, in his Critical Dictionary, giveth certain particulars, and at least one passage whereof hath been thought worthy of imitation by a poet of no lesser note than Mr. John Milton.

In the meanwhile, referring those who list to know more of the writer to other authorities, some judgment of the man may be formed from observing the old saw as to the company he kept. In all the collected editions of his works there is printed a letter to him, written by Pico of Mirandola, from Florence, dated September 19, 1490, in which the much-praised Pico liberally praiseth Baptist for his poems, and desireth him to salute "our Beroaldus." " If you have done," addeth he, "with Philostratus on the life of Apollonius, I should be glad to have it, as well as the copy of Zacharias the Philosopher you tell me you picked up at Rome. Remember, too, some time to let me have the catalogue of your library at Bologna." To this letter Mantuan gleefully replieth at the beginning of October, saying that he hath lent the Philostratus to Beroaldus, and desiring to be remembered by Pico to Politian, at Florence. Correspondence of this kind he kept up with many men of letters, and Father Cupaer prints a letter to him, writ from Naples in June, 1499, by Jovian Pontanus. One of his poems, I note also, is addrest to that true Master in painting, Andrea Mantegna, with whom he would seem to have been a familiar. Erasmus, saith Mr. Rose, writeth in praise of our author, but he giveth no reference, and I have not yet fallen on the passage.

But, after all, I know not that any better testimony as to what manner of man he was can be given than that which is to be gathered from this Poem. A certain Joannes Rex, the author of an opuscule he calleth Parthenandria, falleth foul toward the end thereof of *Baptistam illum nostrum Mantuanum*, for that he mixeth profane with sacred things ; and other keen-scented critick noses seem to have snuffed in his works some slight odour of constructive heresy. Trithemius crediteth him with a tractate, *De ortu Religionum*, which I find in no shape among his many works. Methinks, however, a less rigorous inquisitor than John de Torquemada might haply have discovered in this poem certain perilous stuff which, had the author been a less stedfast pillar of the Church in his other works, might have left no ground for the report noticed by Mr. Moreri, that down to his days the body of Mantuan was preserved entire.

His life in the Antwerp edition, *ut supra*, and the references in Moreri ; "Petrus Lucius, Bibl Carm. ; Possevin, Bellarmine ; Tritheme, de Script. Eccl. ; Paul Jove in elog. doct. vir., c. 61 ; Vossius, li. 3, de Hist. Lat. ; Lilio Giraldi, dial. 1 de Poet., sui temp. ; Alegre in Parad. Carmel., &c." All these are to be found boiled down in the Bibliotheca Carmelitana, Orleans, 1752 ; and I learn from Oettinger's Bibliographie Biographique, 2 vols., Brussels, 1854, that there exists "Ambrosi (Florido) Vita di B. Mantovano. Torino, 1785. 8vo." Vol. III.

Biog. Dict., s. v. Mantovano.

Jod. Badius, Paris, 1510.

The Carmelite brother to whom the poem is addrest was in his way quite as noteworthy a personage as the poet himself. John Crestoni of Piacenza, perhaps better known to lexicographers as Janus or Joannes Monachus Placentinus, deserveth to be held in grateful remembrance as the compiler and editor of the first Greek Lexicon printed in the Revival of Letters, the prolific parent of all the Greek Lexicons in common use down at least to the time when Henry Estienne published his ill-fated Treasury of the Greek Tongue. That most famous of the famous family of Stephani, printers of Paris, himself nameth this monk, John of Piacenza, as the first who set hand to the Lexicons then current; and albeit he condemneth the work for sundry shortcomings, and noteth that the explanations of the words are sometimes even given in Italian instead of Latine, still methinks, by his naming the Author, he was minded to imply that he held the good monk of Piacenza worthy of remembrance and gratitude. Mr. Maittaire expressly commendeth him to our thanks, not indeed for his Lexicon, but for a Greek and Latin Psalter which he also edited a few years later, in 1481. No place, year, nor printer is named in the Lexicon, but since Denis Paravisini certainly printed, in 1476, the Greek Grammar writ by Constantine Lascaris, and probably also Crestoni's Psalter in 1481, 'tis most like that Crestoni's Lexicon issued from the same press at Milan sometime between these two dates, about 1478 belike, as the lettering runs on the sumptuous copy in the Bodleian.

Where Crestoni gat his Greek I do not find, but 'tis far from unlikely that his teacher may have been Theodore Gaza, who came to Italy after the Turk took Thessalonica in 1430, and learnt Latine at Mantua. Aldus Manutius saith that Pico of Mirandola and Angelo Politian, among others he nameth, learnt their Greek from Gaza's translation of Aristotle Of Animals, so that a third friend of Mantuan's may well have drawn his Greek from the same source. Philip Beroaldus, also, I judge from his praises of this Theodore, owed to him some part of his knowledge. If we may account Theodore as the friend or teacher of Crestoni and Mantuan, then were they friends of the only three men among the restorers of Letters in Italy of whom Joseph Scaliger proclaimed himself envious, to wit, Gaza, Pico of Mirandola, and Politian.

al. Chrestoni, Crastoni, and Chrastoni.

In his letter to his friends about his Thesaurus in 1560, reprinted in Theod. Janason de Vitis Stephanorum, Ant., 1683, p. 156.

Annal. Typogr. I., 140.

Auct. O., infra II., 3.

There were sundry others, however, of whom Crestoni might have learnt. George the Cretan, who called himself of Trebizonde, was teaching in 1473 at Venice, to which state Cardinal Bessarion gave his library, containing many Greek MSS., in 1468. The elder Argyropylus, who taught Politian in Aristotle's philosophy, died in the very year 1478, and in the next year Lorenzo de' Medici invited Demetrius Chalcondylas to succeed him at Florence. He was driven thence, 'tis said, by the *sæva ambitio* of Politian, and went to Milan, where he published the first edition of Suidas' Greek Dictionary in 1499, more than 20 years later than this Lexicon of Crestoni.

Yet another Greek there was in Italy in those days, a poet of some note, who, if he were the bitter enemy of Politian, one of Mantuan's friends, was yet the friend and disciple of another friend, Jovian Pontanus. This was Michael Marullus, the Tarchaniote, who, driven from Constantinople when that city was taken by the Turk in 1453, had found a home in Italy. Of him Beatus Rhenanus, not without cause, complaineth that he was verily heathenish, and in his poems did venerate the Pagan Gods. Whether Crestoni had any of his Greek from Marullus there is nought to show, yet Mantuan, methinks, may haply have acquired from him something of the gentle heathenishness of this poem, which 'twere evil-speaking to call heretical in one whose religion in truth would seem to have verged at times closely on enthusiasm.

'Tis not known when Crestoni died, but Trithemius saith in 1492 that he believeth him to be still alive. The same writer speaketh of him as a poet, and referreth to certain verses of his printed in Crucejus' Edition of Callimachus' hymns. Crucejus himself saith that he was as good a Grecian as Demetrius Chalcondylas; and Philelphus hath also recorded his high opinion of his parts and attainments. See Bibl. Carm., Orleans, 1752; also Tiraboschi, Ed. Modena, 1790, VI., 836, end of part 2. The Ven. Dr. Hody de Græcis, &c., London, 1742.

Such, then, is the good Carmelite Brother John, to whom the good Carmelite Brother Baptist biddeth God-speed in these verses following. Crestoni is just starting, from Bologna I take it, to Monte Calestano, some 16 miles from the City of Parma, on the river so named, a hill, saith the writer of his life, most pleasant from its passing wholesome air and the delightsomeness of the situation. I know not on what occasion he went on this pleasant pilgrimage, yet it may well be that it Bibl. Carm., t. n. Crestoni.

was for needed rest and recreation after seeing his Lexicon through the Press ; for the compilation and editing of the first Greek Lexicon, be it never so faulty and jejune, is a work that might well have wearied a Titan. At his going Mantuan will bid him farewell in Latin elegiacks, and of a certainty I think it may be said, never before had thoughts such as are here expressed smouldered under the scapularies of St. Simon Stock. The sympathetic brace of White Friars, 'tis clear, like honey-bees in spring-tide among the first blossoms of wild thyme on Hybla, are excellently—nay, ecstatically—drunken on the supernacular secret honey of the buds of Greek Letters just beginning to blow under the genial showers, soft winds, and warm sunshine of the Intellectual New Birth of the World.

I will here only add that my translation, done in the jog-trot ballad metre of old Master Turberville in his version of the Eclogues, hath been made from a copy of an edition of Mantuan apparently unknown to our bibliographers. The title runneth :

Prima Pars operū

Baptistę Mantuani : in qua sunt

Alphonsus, Triumphus. Panęgyris

Roberti sanseverinatis & Syluæ.

[Prelū Ascensianū.]

Venūdatur in vico

sancti Iacobi in ædibus Ascensianis :

& sub Pelicano.

All the type, save the words *Prima Pars* and *Venūdatur*, is printed in rubrick, and the words *Prelū Ascensianū* are on a label attached to the printing-press of which a cut is given. 'Tis in 8vo, unpaged, but registered from A to Xx., 704 pp., in 44 sheets. The colophon readeth : ſ

Finis Ex ædibus Ascensianis Nonis
Septembris. MDVII.

Whether the second and any farther part of this Edition were ever printed I know not. The poem begins on Vv. 8 v., and forms part of the 7th book of the Sylvæ or Miscellanies. There is a note at the beginning of the 3rd book of the Sylvæ, to the effect. that the Panegyrick on Robert of Sanseverino, which theretofore had formed the 3rd book, had been separately printed, so that what had been the 4th book is here the 3rd. In some former edition, therefore, this poem is probably to be found in the 8th and not the 7th book of the Sylvæ, though it appears in the 7th in the Antwerp, and, I infer, in all subsequent editions to this of 1507. This book is remarkable as being the earliest by some months in which the print of the Ascensian Press appears.

I assume in the collected edition of his works, printed at Bologna in 1502, but I have never seen it.

TO JOHN CRESTONI, CARMELITE, WHO COMPOSED THE LEXICON, THAT IS, THE GREEK VOCABULARY.

Go forth! The pleasant uplands range of Calestano's hill ;
With happy luck go forth, and home return with happier still !
And if the mountain-haunting Fauns or Pan thou chance to see,
Greet them, I pray, and in my name say these few words from me :

"Ye Deities, who nought have now beyond an empty name—
Which sure our grandsires old had held a foul and grievous shame—
Answer me this, nor grudge awhile to list to what I say,
For all the question here I ask will breed no long delay :—
When all the world the Roman won and ruled in elder days,
Then mighty was the store of Gods and mighty was their praise :
Then, greatest, Jupiter did haunt the topmost citadels,
And held his see Capitoline aloft among the fells ;
Then to the folk that counsel craved Phœbus gave answer true,
And bore his rank among the Gods to whom was worship due ;
Thou, Mavors, too, wert great, for they who did the City found
Were both from thy advoutry sprung, the Brother-twins renowned ;
And Venus, Lady of the Seas, Youth's goddess, Mars his joy,
Herself was Mother then of Love, the quiver-bearing boy :

Her roaming once Anchises found and pressed on Simois' banks of old,
And did Æneas then beget, as ancient songs have told;
Pallas, whose Gorgon ægis walled her breast inviolate,
Was Godhead mid the Godheads then and great among the great:
The first discoverer She of all the Arts, men said
Sprang forth a daughter from the womb of Jove's own sacred head;
Then, too, the witless common folk made Maia's son a God,
The winged poster Mercury, who wields the sleepy rod;
Then Mulciber in Ætna's lairs his lightning forge did ply,
Who fashioned arms he gave to Jove, the Sovran of the sky;
The mighty Mother of the Gods then royally did tread
With brazen towers and girdling moles around her reverend head;
And to Dircæan Bacchus still men brought the choicest dues,
For that the God did eloquence and mirth of heart infuse;
Far-famous Vesta, too, of her undying flame was glad,
Who on thy margent, Albula, her neighbour temple had;
Fair Cynthia did a-hunting go by shady forest trees,
Her gentle battle-fields, and brought the swift-foot Goddesses;
The Tiber-haunting Janus' gate a blessed peace did bar,
But open Janus evermore stood wide in time of war:
Then all this Universe was shared by the Saturnian seed,
Which right and law to sea and land and Gods above decreed.

" Say wherefore faded from the Gods their sovranty away ?
What Power among these powers above could be more strong than they ?
Ah, mortal men, how many things we wot not of there be!
This earthy flesh afflicts our sprites so that we cannot see!
While you, ye Gods, round whose calm minds no fleshly cloud is rolled,
With clearest-sighted eyes do all this changing world behold.

Of giant-bulk, so poets tell, the earthborn Brethren strove
Erstwhile a mortal war to wage against the Gods above;
But He, the Sire, with driving bolts and mountains huge down-hurled
Flashed fire upon those warriors bold and scathed them from the world.
Still, proudly fain, the wit of man would scale the skiey walls,
Yet on the baffled schemer's head for aye the vengeance falls.
The o'erweening subtlety that wrought Prometheus' priceless theft
Full many a grievous rankling wound on humankind hath left,
For whatsoever fell disease doth mortal frailty wring
Had in that ancient crime of his its origin and spring:
Say then what lordly Power was that which durst so dread a deed?
Such work methinks than mortal man's a mightier hand would need.

" Mars hath no sword; the spear no more doth shake in Pallas' hand;
Phœbus, I ween, hath lost his harp, and Jove his levin-brand.
Their lofty temples on the ground lie low, nor lives the man
Who doth with Tuscan wizardry the victim's entrails scan.
The elder world Priapus did of ill conditions feign,
To whom not even an altar now nor effigies remain:
All garments cast aside himself the Deity displayed,
And for the lewd rout passing by a laughing-stock was made.
Who knows not Isis and the pomp of all her rites of yore?
Yet men in Memphis know her not, she Goddess is no more.
Say then what lordly Power was that which durst so dread a deed?
Such work methinks than mortal man's a mightier hand would need.

" 'Twas Christ the mighty, when He left the Olympian skies behind,
Who thus, 'tis said, ye Gods of old, prevailed against your kind;
And meet to hold that wondrous work for His alone we deem,
For many a wondrous deed He wrought, worthy the God supreme:
He from the accursed Serpent reft the fangs that bit so deep,
And did to death with venomed plague the Lord's own holy sheep;
He with His arrows pierced and quelled the swelling Python's pride,
A beast more pestilent and fell than all on earth that bide;
With tidings of salvation He man's feeble heart made strong,
Gave law to human foolishness, set bounds to human wrong;
He for the darkness of the world created a new sun,
And bade the obedient stars of heaven in a new orbit run.
More wary and more valiant He than mighty Hercules,
Scared with almighty hand the black Tartarean fastnesses;
He with His hell-compelling words the den Cerberean cleft,
And of his choicest conqueror-spoil the sable King bereft:
O'er Dis in this wise triumphed He, and from the margent dread
Of Styx below to heavenly realms the reverend Fathers led;
Recalled the life that fleeting once had left the anatomy,
And mortal sons of mortals made twice live and twice made die.

" We, seeing then these wondrous deeds the Virgin's Only Son,
Even as our fathers testify, in elder time hath done,
We are persuaded to believe, ye Gods, that His the might
Before the which your smitten backs ye gave to headlong flight.
If He indeed your conqueror was, to Orcus hie ye then,
There where the water ever burns in Styx's fiery fen !
Why thus with glozing names beguile a world so hard to teach,
Make mock of honest ignorance, our grosser wits o'er-reach ?

But if what to our sprites befals be only not to know,
And otherwise the truth may be than that we fancy so,
Show then your light, and point us out where we have gone astray,
And help us lest in such a night again we miss our way.
Again let build your temples then, your altars rise once more,
And haste we then your ancient fame and worship to restore !
Tarpeianwards Mevania let send her bulls of snow,
And night-black let the victim be that bleeds to Jove below !
To Ceres let her swine be burnt ; his kid to Bacchus kill,
That he in turn with joyous must our vintage-vats may fill !
To every God his offering due, and all their altars heap !
Loud let the priestly trumpet blare, and bright the flame-tongues leap !
And to all gods of sea or land, or high Olympus' bound,
Let the long double pipe again its gladsome discord sound ! "

On this wise to those ancient Gods I pray thee speak for me,
If any a one beneath a rock in pilgriming thou see ;
And, as thou lov'st me, bring me back truly his answer all,
And of thine own to grace the same, sweet verses therewithal.
Bid hail the country side for me, its joyous tilths and trees,
Proud of their fresh young leaves, and all the birds' sweet melodies ;
Bid hail the vine-clad hills, the figs, the olive-clumps, and greet
The many-coloured fields and banks whose garments smell so sweet !
And when the blushing dawn hath chased the darkness from the sky,
Awake, nor let thy lusty limbs in sluggard slumber lie !
The watchful linnet then through all the fields renews her lay,
And gladly welcomes with her trill the pleasant coming day.
Up, then, and ransack all the plots the garden-rills between
And grassy banks beyond with all the cool Spring's freshness green ;

Gather the spearmint's flowery spikes upsprouting fresh and strong,
And wild-thyme's treasure newly sprung the straggling tufts among,
The lad's-love and the wormwood's hair, the feathery fennel tall,
With basil and sweet marjoram and pullein therewithal;
With thumb-nail shielded from the thorn, the hedge-row roses reave,
And all the spoil with cunning hand in dewy garlands weave!
Go forth! The pleasant uplands range of Calestano's hill;
With happy luck go forth, and home return with happier still!